Precious Waste

Waste not
Want not!

Neil Griffiths

Illustrated by Janette Louden

Rewarding Learning

Meet Ryan, a refuse collector who was different.

Unlike most refuse collectors, Ryan simply hated collecting rubbish! It wasn't that Ryan was lazy, in fact, he was always working hard, making his daily collections. No, the problem for Ryan was that he simply hated throwing things away.

As a boy, his mum had told him, "Waste not want not!" and his dad was always saying, "I'm sure we can use that for something". At first, Ryan didn't quite know what his parents had meant, but as he grew up, he began to realise that just as his dad had said, almost everything you might think of throwing away could be put to good use again.

PLASTIC BAGS

COMPOST

ALUMINIUM & GLASS

PAPER

ICE CREAM

ICE

A visit to Ryan's house was proof of that! Can you spot his handy recycling?

Ryan's mum's words had also proved to be true, as Ryan very rarely needed to buy anything. So being a refuse collector wasn't easy for Ryan as he would get so cross at the amount of useful things people threw away. In fact, most evenings, Ryan could be found sorting through the rubbish for things to reuse.

On Saturdays, he would then take his refuse lorry to the local 'Recycling Centre' and drop off paper for pulping, cans for crushing, bottles to be bashed and rags for ripping, all to be made ready for recycling.

But not everyone was like Ryan, and on one particular day, his patience finally ran out.

As his lorry drew up early one morning in the High Street of Lisbogey, the sight before him was just too much! The street was piled higher than ever with sacks and sacks of so-called rubbish. Ryan knew it was time for him to do something about it.

LISBOGEY
TOWN HALL

HOTEL

LI

POST
OFFICE

Outside the Town Hall, he counted twelve sacks full of shredded paper in their wheelie bins. Why were they throwing so much away? he thought. Ryan decided to investigate as he had always been quite curious about what went on inside the Town Hall.

Next, Ryan set off for the hotel, where he found bags and bags of paper cups and bottles. Ryan hadn't ever been into a big hotel before, and he was rather nervous. He had always stayed in a Bed and Breakfast during his holidays to the seaside.

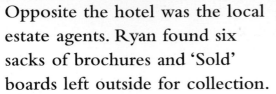

Opposite the hotel was the local estate agents. Ryan found six sacks of brochures and 'Sold' boards left outside for collection.

Once inside, Ryan could see lots of photos of houses. There was office equipment everywhere. A nice lady asked Ryan if she could help him.

Whilst Ryan had yet another cup of tea, he told the nice lady that card and paper could be pulped and made into new packaging. He asked her if she could save some of the paper, as the local school could use it to draw and write on the back of. Before leaving, he told the lady how their ink cartridges could be refilled. The nice lady thanked Ryan for all his help.

By now, Ryan had drunk rather too much tea and popped into the post office to use their lavatory! He had to climb over sackfuls of used envelopes, receipts and leaflets.

As Ryan was leaving, he spotted George, the owner of the garage, posting a parcel, so he walked out with him. He talked about the stacks of tyres and oil cans he'd left for collection.

He had often wondered about who worked in the newspaper offices. Ryan liked the staff of the Lisbogey News a lot, as they always seemed to be so careful and left little rubbish to be collected. Today there was only one bag with old tea bags and stale cakes and sandwiches in it.

EDITOR

LISBOGEY N

Inside, Ryan saw the busy printing presses, and was taken to the editor's office.

This time it was Ryan who was to learn a lot. The editor told Ryan that the newspaper was printed on recycled paper, and all their paper waste went for recycling. Ryan congratulated her, but said that tea bags and food waste thrown out by their canteen would make excellent compost.

Ryan noticed that Flora from the florist and nursery had placed an advert in the paper, so he thought he would call in to see her next.

There were eight sacks full of cuttings outside her shop. Ryan couldn't find Flora anywhere, but she finally emerged from a mass of greenery.

Ryan admired all Flora's flowers and told her that the bedding plants he had bought from her were doing very well in his garden.

He handed Flora a booklet on how to make compost from old garden cuttings and kitchen waste. Flora thought this was an excellent idea, and would save her money buying in compost. She gave Ryan a lovely bunch of flowers to thank him.

At the end of the High Street, Ryan passed an empty shop and pulled up outside the Tourist Information Office. He was disappointed to find five sacks of old leaflets waiting to be collected. But they gave Ryan another idea.

TO LET

OPEN

TOURIST
INFORMATION

Once inside, Ryan was glad he had made the visit, as he discovered so much about the local area he lived in.

The Information Officer was really helpful and told Ryan lots about the town. Ryan hadn't realised that Lisbogey was twinned with another town called Delaroo.

Ryan then told her about the Recycling Centre and asked if the Tourist Information Office would put up a poster and give out leaflets to visitors.

The officer was really keen to help and said she would take all their old leaflets to be recycled from now on.

Ryan drove off in his lorry feeling very satisfied with his day's work. He left behind him a busy High Street, full of people who now knew a lot more about reusing and recycling.

Several days later, Ryan arrived for his usual collection and was given a huge surprise!
There was hardly any rubbish to collect. The folks in the High Street had indeed been busy!
Everyone had listened to Ryan, and now there was hardly a rubbish sack in sight!

The Town Hall had delivered their shredded paper to the post office to use as packaging for fragile packages.

The hotel had given Flora all their paper cups to sow her seedlings in, and the newspaper offices had taken over their tea bags and canteen waste for Flora's compost.

The post office were now reusing all their envelopes, and George had donated lots of his tyres to make raised flower beds along the High Street. Flora had already planted up a few and they certainly made the High Street look a prettier place.

The Tourist Information Office had kept their word and taken their old leaflets to be recycled, and Ryan could see a recycling poster in the front window. It seemed that everyone had become keen to recycle better.

The Mayor spotted Ryan's lorry and rushed over excitedly. He said the Chamber of Commerce were meeting the next day and would like Ryan to be guest of honour.

The following evening, Ryan spoke at a packed meeting. Everyone was there and they were full of ideas. George also spoke on behalf of the community, saying they must do more to recycle. The Tourist Information Office had contacted their twin town and found out what they did.

They used oil drums for charcoal burners and melted tyres down to put soles on new slippers. Flora and George thought the burners were a brilliant idea and said they could sell them in the nursery.

The manager of the hotel said he would be keen to buy slippers that used recycled rubber, to leave for residents to wear in their rooms.

The newspaper editor had written an article in the paper and asked for ideas and had received hundreds of suggestions.

The Chief Executive of the Chamber of Commerce finally stood up and congratulated everyone on the progress they had made so far. He announced that a special Recycling Day would be planned to promote the initiative. Everyone cheered, especially Ryan. He said, "One business's rubbish could be another business's treasure!" They cheered even louder.

Later that month, a wonderful Recycling Day was held in the High Street.

The hotel provided outside catering, the Tourist Information Office gave out leaflets, George and Flora gave demonstrations on making compost and burners.

But the best part of the day was saved until last, when Ryan was asked to step forward and pull a cord which unveiled a dazzling new refuse lorry with sections for recycling and a brand new uniform for Ryan.
The newspaper's photographer covered the whole event and Ryan was front cover news!

What a day!

LISBOGEY NEWS

75P

June 26th

GLASS PAPER

BIN 2

Ryan, Lisbogey's local refuse collector, standing in front of his new recycling lorry

Recycling Ryan

...day saw the launch of Lisbogey's first ... Ryan is the refuse collector behind ... weeks ago when

he began a campaign to encourage High Street residents to recycle and re-use the items they would normally throw in the rubbish.

But all the excitement didn't change Ryan. He still did his collections (although there was less to collect!) as he always did, but he had taken on another little 'side-line', he had opened a shop in the High Street, which sold things Ryan had made from waste.

Now all Ryan is looking for is a name for his shop.

To find out more about ways to recycle and help the environment, log-on to the following websites:

www.recycling-guide.org.uk

www.recycle-more.co.uk

www.recyclezone.org.uk

www.olliesworld.com/uk

www.ecofriendlykids.co.uk

www.clean-air-kids.org.uk

www.wastewatch.org.uk

Please note that the Publisher is not responsible for the content of these websites and that the information and views expressed on them does not necessarily reflect those of the publisher.

Published by
Storysack Limited
Resource House, Kay Street, Bury BL9 6BU, UK

ISBN 978-1-904949-15-2

Text © Neil Griffiths 2008
Illustrations © Janette Louden 2008
First published in the UK 2008

The right of Neil Griffiths to be identified as the author of this work has been asserted by him in accordance with the Copyright, Designs and Patents Act 1988.

Design by David Rose

Printed by Tien Wah Press Pte. Ltd., Malaysia

This book has been printed on paper from a sustainable source.